# SUNBIRD

Published by Ladybird Books Ltd 2012
A Penguin Company
Penguin Books Ltd, 80 Strand, London, WC2R ORL, UK
Penguin Group (USA) Inc., 375 Hudson Street, New York 10014, USA
Penguin Books Australia Ltd, Camberwell Road, Camberwell, Victoria 3124,
Australia (A division of Pearson Australia Group Pty Ltd)
Penguin Group (NZ), 67 Apollo Drive, Rosedale, Auckland 0632,
New Zealand (a division of Pearson New Zealand Ltd)
Canada, India, South Africa

Sunbird is a trade mark of Ladybird Books Ltd

Written by Kieran Grant (except competition winners where stated)
Illustrated by Vincent Béchet, Fran and David Brylewska, Nik Holmes and Lea Wade.
© Mind Candy Ltd. Moshi Monsters is a trademark
of Mind Candy Ltd. All rights reserved.

All rights reserved. No part of this publication may be reproduced, stored in a retrieval system,
or transmitted in any form or by any means, electronic, mechanical, photocopying, recording
or otherwise, without the prior consent of the copyright owner.

www.ladybird.com

ISBN: 978-1-40939-0961
001 - 10 9 8 7 6 5 4 3 2 1
Printed in Slovakia

# Moshi Monsters™

## Monsterific Comic Collection

# MOSHI PIT

IN FLUTTERBY FOREST . . .

I'M SURE I SAW A LESSER SPOTTED GREEN TRICKSTER FLY INTO THESE WOODS!

IF I CATCH IT I'LL BE THE TOAST OF THE FLUTTERBY CLUB!

THERE IT IS! COME BACK, LITTLE FELLOW!

WHAT THE?!

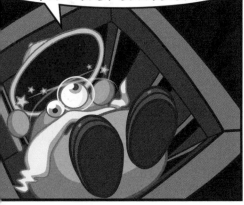

# Time to Reflect

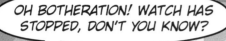

# What Goes on in a Moshling's Mind?

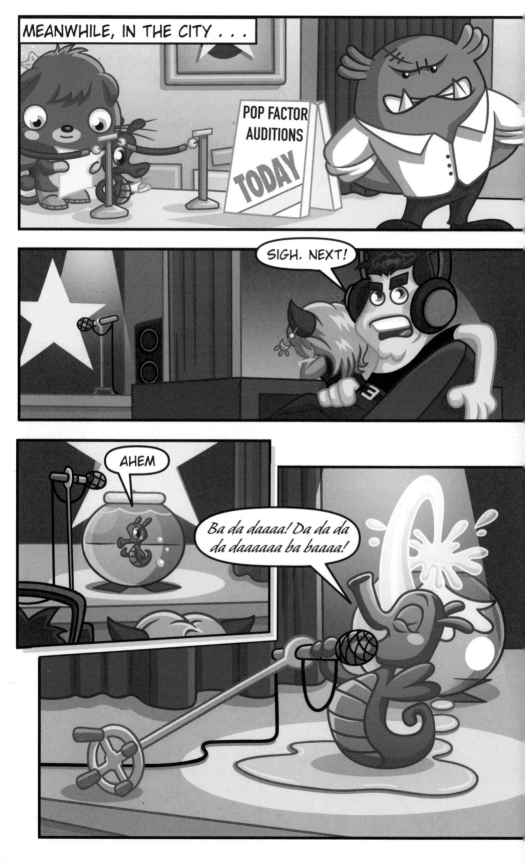

FURI'S FOOD FIGHT

Runner-Up: mari33

# Raiders of the Lost Air Con!

# Beneath the Ice-cano

# THE BALLAD OF CAP'N BUC.

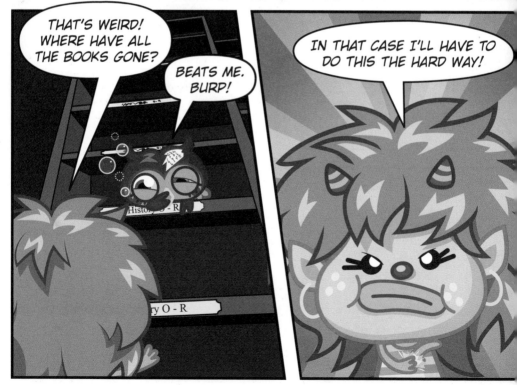

# Create Your Own Comics

Paint on your moustaches and put on your berets, because it's time to get artistic and have a go at making your own comics! Grab some blank paper and colouring pens or pencils and follow Furi's top tips!

- Don't try to fit too much into your pictures or words. Keep it simple!

- Just tell one joke or short story. And make it funny!

- Lots of the humour in comic strips is in the pictures. You might not even need words!

- Have fun and don't forget to share your comics!